ID0606254

RECEIVED

NOV 09 2017

Douglass-Truth Branch Library

ISBN-13: 978-0-8249-5687-5

Published by WorthyKids/Ideals
An imprint of Worthy Publishing Group
A division of Worthy Media, Inc.
Nashville, Tennessee

Copyright © 2017 by Katherine Schwarzenegger

All rights reserved. No part of this publication may be reproduced or transmitted in any form
or by any means, electronic or mechanical, including photocopy, recording, or any information
storage and retrieval system, without permission in writing from the publisher.

WorthyKids/Ideals is a registered trademark of Worthy Media, Inc.

Library of Congress CIP data on file

Designed by Georgina Chidlow-Irvin
Edited by Pamela Kennedy

Printed and bound in the U.S.A.
LBP_Jul17_1

For all those who open their hearts and their homes to animals in
need, and for my Maverick, who taught me how to love big.

— K.S.

To my greatest loves and supporters—my husband, Brad;
my daughter, Emily; and Ron and Eliana.

— P.H.

KATHERINE SCHWARZENEGGER

Maverick and Me

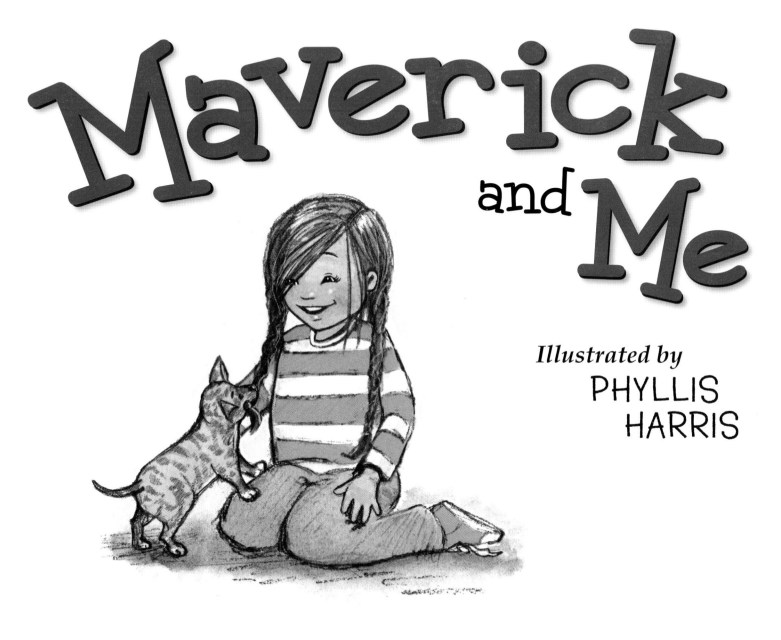

Illustrated by
PHYLLIS HARRIS

Worthy **kids**
ideals®

Nashville, Tennessee

Dear Parents and Dog Lovers,

Maverick and Me is based on a true story—the story of my own rescue dog.

I became involved in animal rescue several years ago when I started fostering puppies. Just when I decided to take a break, I was asked to foster one more—Maverick. He came to me as a very sick two-and-a-half-week-old puppy who had been found under a freeway. Over the weeks of nursing him back to health, I fell in love. And soon, I no longer needed to find a home for Maverick—he was home, with me.

I wrote this story to be a voice for the millions of dogs (and cats!) looking for homes each year. My hope is that the book sparks a conversation among children and their families about animals in need. And when the time comes to bring a dog into your home, I hope that you might choose to adopt.

In addition to fostering and adopting, there are many ways to help homeless animals:

- Hold a dog-food or cat-food drive.
- Collect old towels and sheets for local shelters.
- Volunteer at a local shelter. Many allow children (with a parent or guardian) to walk dogs or play with cats.
- Share the idea of pet adoption with family and friends who are looking for a new pet.
- Connect with local shelters and rescue groups about how you can help animals in your community.

I hope you enjoy *Maverick and Me* as much as I enjoyed writing it—and as much as I enjoy my own real-life Maverick!

XO,
Katherine

It was a cold and rainy afternoon. Maverick shivered as cars sped by overhead, splashing dirty water. He whimpered and his tummy growled. He was scared and lonely.

"Hey there, little fellow."

Maverick's heart pounded. A hand reached down and pulled him from the muddy puddle. The frightened puppy squeezed his eyes shut. But as gentle arms wrapped around him, Maverick dared to peek. He saw a smiling face.

Exhausted, he cuddled into the
folds of the soft coat and fell asleep.

"Poor little guy," the woman said to the manager of the pet supply store. "I found him under the freeway, all alone and shivering."

The manager nodded and stroked Maverick's muddy, matted fur. He filled a bowl with food and put it down.

Maverick wriggled free and stuck his nose into the dish. Nothing had ever tasted so yummy.

"Slow down, little fellow," laughed the manager.

"I'd like to help him find a good home," the woman said.

"We have a pet adoption event next weekend," replied the manager. "If you can take care of him and help him get stronger, you can bring him to the event. Maybe we can find him a home."

Pet adoption
Next weekend

Saturday 10-4
Sunday 1-4

"Great idea!" said the woman. She bought some puppy food and a chew toy for Maverick.

"Come on, little guy," she said, scooping him up. "Let's see if we can get you ready for a family of your own!"

When the weekend of the adoption event arrived, Maverick couldn't wait to find his new family. His coat was brushed and shiny, and his eyes sparkled with excitement.

ADOPT ME!

Champ

ADOPT ME!

Percy

The manager of the store gave
him a kennel close to the front, next
to a big, fluffy yellow dog and a smaller,
black-and-white dog.

Whenever someone came near,
Maverick wiggled and wagged his tail,
but no one seemed to notice him.

A little boy glanced at Maverick and shouted, "Look, Daddy! A puppy!" Then he quickly ran over to the big, fluffy yellow dog and said, "I want this one, Daddy!"

But his dad replied, "You already have two hamsters! Let's go."

A little girl peeked into Maverick's kennel and smiled. "You're a funny-looking little pup," she said. Then she saw a dog with a bow and said, "I think I like you best!"

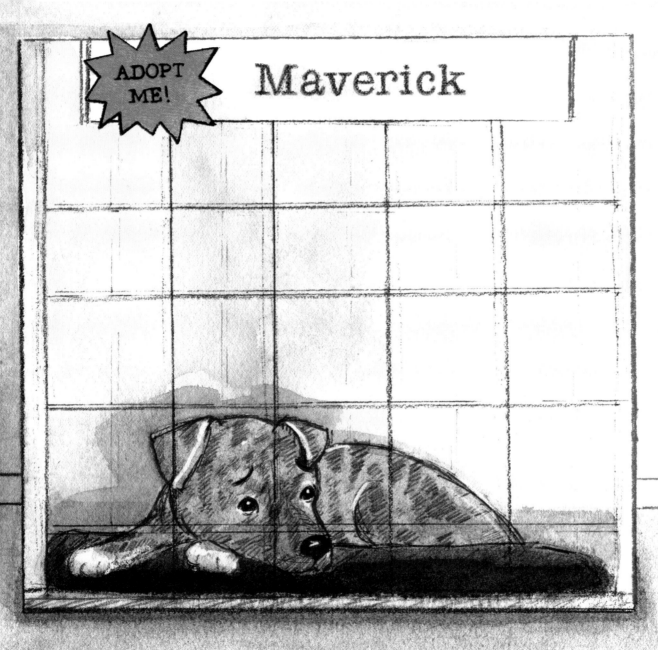

As closing time approached, Maverick was the only dog that hadn't been adopted. He wanted to believe that he would find a home, but it was getting harder and harder to be hopeful. His little ears drooped.

The store manager walked by. "Sorry, little guy. Maybe you'll have better luck next weekend."

Just then, a little girl with pigtails and freckles walked in with her mom. "Now, Scarlett, let's see how quickly we can find a present for Nena's cat," Scarlett's mother said.

Maverick perked up. This looked like a friendly little girl! He tried to act well behaved. He sat up straight. He cocked his head to one side. But she didn't notice.

He wagged his tail
and ran around in circles,
but the little girl started
to walk past him.

Oh, no! he
thought. Maverick
yipped and bounced
up and down.

Scarlett turned. "Mama, look! I've never seen a dog like this. He looks like a marble. And look at his ears!"

Scarlett ran to Maverick's kennel. "Can I hold him?" she asked.

The store manager opened the kennel, and Scarlett sat down next to Maverick. He climbed into her lap. Scarlett laughed. "Mama, he's so cute. And he loves me!"

ADOPT ME!

Maverick

"Oh, Scarlett. You know we're not here to look for a puppy today."

"But Mama, look! This sign says 'Adopt Me!' He has no family."

"That's right!" the manager said. "Someone found this little guy all alone and sick. His name is Maverick. He's healthy now, but he needs a forever-home. All the dogs that were here today needed homes and families."

"See, Mama?" Scarlett said. "He needs us!" She giggled as Maverick tugged one of her braids.

Scarlett's mother frowned. "I don't know."

Just then, Maverick reached out and put a little paw on her arm.

She laughed. "He certainly is sweet! But Scarlett, having a dog is a big job."

"I'll help take care of him, Mama. Please, I promise," pleaded Scarlett.

Scarlett's mom looked at Scarlett, then Maverick. She could see that they had already fallen in love. "Well," she said with a smile, "I guess we have a new family member."

Scarlett squealed and hugged Maverick. She nestled her nose into his soft fur and whispered in his ear, "Let's go home, Maverick."

Scarlett chose a leash and collar. Her mother bought puppy food, and they led Maverick out the door.

Once they got home,
Scarlett dashed up the stairs
to make a bed for Maverick.

He dove into the
closet, then peeked out.

"Silly Maverick!" laughed Scarlett. "I'm so glad you're mine! I can't wait for my friends to meet you. I want to tell them all about puppies just like you that need homes. We're going to help so many dogs!"

Then Scarlett had an idea. She would throw a party! She made invitations for everyone she knew.

Welcome to the Family
Party for
Maverick!

Scarlett and her mom made lemonade and baked cupcakes. Maverick helped!

Scarlett decorated her backyard with balloons and streamers. Maverick helped!

Scarlett's friends and neighbors gathered for the party. She held Maverick and told the story of his rescue and adoption—and about all the other dogs just like Maverick that needed homes too. Maverick beamed with pride.

Everyone said
hello to Maverick.

He ran . . .

and
cuddled . . .

and licked with his
soft, pink tongue.

"He's the cutest puppy ever!" said Rosemary. "When we get a dog, I want to adopt too!"

"Me too!" Alex said. "I just love his crooked ears and his tiger-looking coat!"

After the party, Scarlett and
Maverick sat on the back porch.
"Oh, Maverick, I love you so much!"
Scarlett said. "We're going to have
so much fun together!

"And maybe, because of you, lots of other puppies will find their own forever-homes. In fact, I'm sure of it!"

Maverick snuggled into Scarlett's
arms. He knew that the very best
thing in the whole wide world
was to have a home and
family where he was loved . . .

FOREVER.